A VERY SPECIAL SNOWFLAKE

By Don Hoffman

Illustrated by Todd Dakins

Story and Text by Don Hoffman
Illustrated by Todd Dakins

Text and Illustrations Copyright © 2016, Don Hoffman

www.averyspecialsnowflake.com • www.peekaboopublishing.com

Peek-A-Boo Publishing
Part of the Peek-A-Boo Publishing Group

Second Edition 2016 • Printed by Shenzhen TianHong Printing Co., Ltd. in Shenzhen, China

ISBN: 978-1-943154-24-1 (Hardback)
ISBN: 978-1-943154-01-2 (Paperback)
ISBN: 978-1-943154-22-7 (eBook)
ISBN: 978-1-943154-21-0 (PDF)
ISBN: 978-1-943154-37-1 (Mobi Pocket)

10 9 8 7 6 5 4 3 2

In memory of my mother, Cora,
who taught me the importance of
kindness, compassion, and hard work
—D.H.

To my wife, the lovely Susan
—T.D.

On the day of the big snowstorm, Jeff and Veronica were playing with their new puppy, Snowflake.

Veronica glanced out the window. "It's like a winter wonderland out there," she said.

"Let's take Snowflake outside!" said Jeff. "We can play in the snow!"

They bundled up in their snowsuits and dashed out the door.

Soft snowflakes whirled all around them. They were as white and fluffy as the puppy's fur.

Snowflake barked with excitement and dove into a snowbank! Jeff and Veronica saw her tail peeking out of the white snow. Then, suddenly, she was gone!

"Where is Snowflake?" cried Veronica.
"We have to find her!"

Their neighbor was shoveling the sidewalk. "Mrs. Bigsby!" they called. "Have you seen Snowflake?"

Mrs. Bigsby stopped shoveling. "Goodness, what are you talking about? I can't keep up with all these snowflakes. There are so many of them!"

Jeff and Veronica looked at each other. They shrugged and ran on to ask someone else.

Their friend the florist pulled up in his truck. He was carrying a large bouquet. "Mr. James!" they called to him. "Have you seen Snowflake?"

Mr. James was busy protecting his flowers from the storm. "I've got to keep moving, kids. All these snowflakes will freeze my prize roses!"

Jeff and Veronica looked at each other. They sighed and ran on.

Next they spotted the neighborhood baker.
He was delivering cakes for a party.
"Mr. Ripple!" they called. "Have you seen
Snowflake?"

Mr. Ripple smiled broadly and held up his
cakes. "You bet! These snowflakes have
inspired me! I've decorated all my cakes
with fluffy white icing today!"

Jeff and Veronica looked at each other.
They shook their heads and ran on.

Just up the street, the policewoman was standing at her corner. "Officer Huffy!" they called to her. "Have you seen Snowflake?"

Officer Huffy proudly put her hands on her hips. "Never fear, children!" she shouted. "It's hard for cars to see you with all these snowflakes falling, but I can help you cross the street!"

Jeff and Veronica looked at each other. They giggled and ran on.

The mail carrier came trudging down the
street. She was carrying her heavy mailbag.
"Miss Jane!" they called to her. "Have you
seen Snowflake?"

"Neither rain, nor wind, nor snowflakes
can stop me!" she called back. "Stand aside,
children. I'm off to finish my route!"

"No one understands!" cried Veronica.
"What will we do?"

The children flopped down into a snowbank to rest. They were worried that they might never see their puppy again.

Then, all of a sudden, they noticed a red ball moving near the snowbank. A puppy was pushing it!

"Snowflake!" Veronica exclaimed.
"You've been here all this time!"

"That's not a snowflake. That's a puppy!"
exclaimed their neighbors.

Jeff patted the puppy's head and grinned happily. "This is who we were looking for all along," he explained.

"She is OUR very special Snowflake!"